southern leopard frog

raccoon

green darner

oystercatcher

alligator

great blue heron

pelican

mole crab

bottle-nosed dolphin

herring gull

snowy egret

black skimmer

pygmy sperm whale

common egret

ghost crab

loggerhead

skate

SIMON & SCHUSTER BOOKS FOR YOUNG READERS

An imprint of Simon & Schuster Children's Publishing Division

1230 Avenue of the Americas, New York, New York 10020

SIMON & SCHUSTER BOOKS FOR YOUNG READERS is a trademark of Simon & Schuster.

Book design by Heather Wood. The text for this book is set in Garth Graphic.

Printed in Hong Kong.

10 9 8 7 6 5 4 3 2 1 First Edition

Library of Congress Cataloging-in-Publication Data

Wright-Frierson, Virginia.

An island scrapbook : dawn to dusk on a barrier island / written and illustrated by

Virginia Wright-Frierson.

p.   cm.

Summary : An artist and her daughter explore a North Carolina barrier island

and tell of all they observe during the course of a September day. ISBN 0-689-81563-8

1. Island ecology—North Carolina—Juvenile literature. 2. Barrier islands—North

Carolina—Juvenile literature. [1. Island ecology—North Carolina. 2. Barrier islands—

North Carolina. 3. Ecology. 4. Islands.] I. Title.

QH105.N8W75   1998   508.756′1—dc21   97-17998

FOR MY DAUGHTER AMY who added so beautifully to this book and shared the
discovery of this special island with me. —V.W.-F., Mom

THANK YOU to Dr. James Lanier, Director of the North Carolina Aquarium at Fort Fisher; Stephanie Carter at the
Sea Turtle Program in Wrightsville Beach, North Carolina; my friends at Bald Head Island and the Smith Island
Land Trust; and Heather Wood. The publisher would also like to thank Dr. Jon Evans for his expert help and advice.

A NOTE ABOUT THE ART: The endpapers are linoleum cuts. The rest of the illustrations were done on Arches
hot-pressed watercolor paper with pencil and Winsor & Newton watercolors.

horseshoe crab
by Amy

first edition

An Island Scrapbook

by Virginia Wright-Frierson

Dawn to Dusk on a Barrier Island

ATLANTIC
OCEAN

SALT
MARSH

OUR HOUSE

LOOKOUT TREE

ALLIGATOR POND

MARITIME FOREST

DUNES

SEA TURTLE
NESTING SITES

SHARK TOOTH

ATLANTIC OCEAN

Simon & Schuster
Books For Young Readers

INDIANA

OHIO

PENNSYLVANIA

WEST
VIRGINIA

MD.

KENTUCKY

VIRGINIA

NORTH
CAROLINA

TENNESSEE

SOUTH
CAROLINA

GEORGIA

ALABAMA

FLORIDA

GULF OF
MEXICO

ATLANTIC
OCEAN

Amy and I are awake before dawn on this September morning. It is the last week at our island house until next summer, and we don't want to waste a minute of it. We dress quietly, grab our packs, and slip outside into the cool darkness of the salt marsh.

"The sun!" calls Amy. It is a fingernail sliver, glowing above the distant trees. We unpack our watercolors, brushes, and sketch pads as fast as we can. I paint a tiny study of the sunrise every few minutes until the soft orange light becomes a fireball.

clapper rail - often heard
but rarely seen

Amy

Amy paints one sunrise study with more detail of the fiery sky and choppy water. As we work, we listen to the whisper of the rustling cordgrass, the lapping of the tide, the call of a clapper rail, and the skittering and claw-clicking of fiddler crabs. The warming breezes bring us the rich muddy smell of the salt marsh.

When our paintings are finished, we walk
under the old dock to look at the mudflats
teeming with fiddler crabs and patterned with
the tracks of night-prowling raccoons.

One fiddler threatens us with his huge violin-
shaped claw while the others vanish into their

ale

female

If a male fiddler loses his big claw, the other will grow large. He will grow a new small claw in place of the lost one!

The male fights with the large claw and also waves it to attract a female. He eats by scooping up mud with the small claw, sucking out the nutrients, then discarding the rest in piles of tiny mudballs.

The female can shovel in food with both of her claws.

burrows. In a few hours, the water will reach the high tide mark on the dock piling. The fiddlers will plug up their tunnels with a mud-ball and wait for low tide to return.

goldenrod

wax
myrtle

We decide to walk through the maritime forest
to the ocean. The springy, sandy floor is covered with
acorns, palm fronds, pine cones and needles, grasses,
and poison ivy. This ground cover provides food and
shelter for deer, birds, and other forest animals.

Insects in the maritime forest

mosquito

no-see-ums

deer fly

ticks

horse fly

chigger

ladybird beetle

carpenter ant

(red bug)

cricket

honey bee

cicada

holly

red cedar

laurel oak

Our island is the northernmost range of this sabal or cabbage palm

dogwood

Yaupon

muscadine vine

smilax vine

dwarf palmetto

Live oaks, pines, and magnolias form the canopy of the maritime forest. Their branches can withstand strong winds and salt spray. They are anchored firmly in the sandy soil by their vast root systems.

The dominant tree is the live oak, often draped with Spanish moss.

The tall trees in the canopy protect the more fragile and salt-sensitive plants in the understory: palmettos, young cedars, dogwoods, bays, hollies, and the toothache tree (Hercules' Club). Chewing its leaves or bark numbs the mouth.

Beauty-berry

Amy climbs up into her lookout tree for a bird's-eye view of the rainwater pond where the egrets roost at night.

She counts eight yellow-bellied turtles before they slip underwater. There are deer tracks and more raccoon prints (they look like tiny human handprints). Amy spots a great blue heron, almost as tall as she is, standing as still as a tree on the far bank, waiting to dart after a fish or frog.

reeds
Spartina
sawgrass

We emerge from the forest shade to a beautiful view of the windswept grasses on the dunes, and the sparkling ocean stretching on forever. Pelicans fly low over the waves in a dotted line. We make our way carefully around the patches of sandspurs and prickly pear cactus to the clean, hard-packed sand of the ocean beach. Only shrimpers, fishermen, and shorebirds are out this early.

We walk along, filling our hats with shells, a sand dollar, interesting pieces of driftwood, sea glass, and smoothed, round rocks. There are rows of small fish visible in the cresting waves. We munch on peanut butter crackers and stop often to watch the birds.

Oystercatchers

Oops - We walk too close

sea
oats

yaupon   cedar

yucca

beach grass

pennywort

shark fin shapes

Almost all
of the fins seen
in our waters are
bottle-nosed dolphins
or manta
rays.

I make some quick pencil sketches
of a snowy egret that has flown up
right in front of us. Amy watches
two bottlenose dolphins arching in
and out of the clear water as they
swim past.

A few weeks ago a small hurricane passed over the island. It was not expected to be very strong, so we were not asked to evacuate.

Amy and I were alone in our house. Luckily we live on the marsh side of the island, which is protected by the forest. But we still spent a nearly sleepless night as the winds roared, the house leaked, and the windows were slammed open. Trees cracked and crashed around us and lightning lit up the marsh. The next morning we went outside to explore and take these photos:

Amy being held up by the wind.

Dune erosion on the ocean side of our island. A set of stairs, a T.V., balloon, light bulb, and lots of dead fish washed up on this spot.

A pine tree knocked over during the storm.

Gulls trying to fly in ___ ___ gale.

Amy pulling her sweatshirt over her face to shield it from the blowing sand.

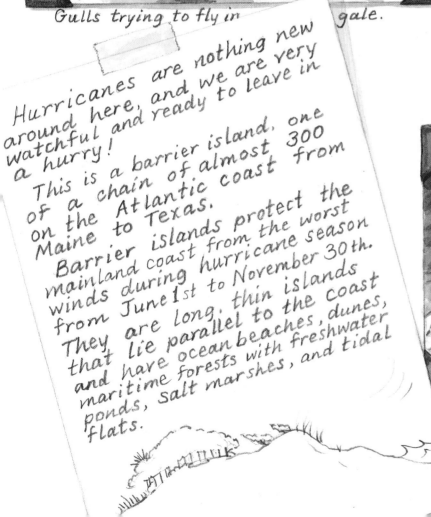

Hurricanes are nothing new around here, and we are very watchful and ready to leave in a hurry!

This is a barrier island, one of a chain of almost 300 on the Atlantic coast from Maine to Texas.

Barrier islands protect the mainland coast from the worst winds during hurricane season from June 1st to November 30th. They are long, thin islands that lie parallel to the coast and have ocean beaches, dunes, maritime forests with freshwater ponds, salt marshes, and tidal flats.

Debris still washing up a week after the hurricane. The ocean around our island is still dark brown from all the flooding of the rivers that feed into it.

Every shell you find on the beach once had a living creature in it. Here are a few:

moon snail

scallop

coquina

angel wing

great heart cockle

sand dollar

great heart cockle

pen shell

oysters

baby's ear

coquinas

razor clam

angel wing

slipper shell

coral

jingle shells (sailor's toenails)

disk shell

moon snail + sand collar

scallops

Some beautiful shells were washed up from the ocean floor during the hurricane. Amy made a collection in an old crate she found.

Now we head back to our house to sort out our treasures on the front porch. Amy has gathered a pile of shiny jingle shells, and also a hat full of ark shells with holes in them for a wind chime.

She has been busy all summer making picture frames and flower pots with glued-on shells, sea glass windows, and a grapevine wreath for our door.

Oyster drills - and moon snails can drill holes into shells to eat the creatures inside.
Shipworms - burrow into driftwood (and boats, piers, and pilings).

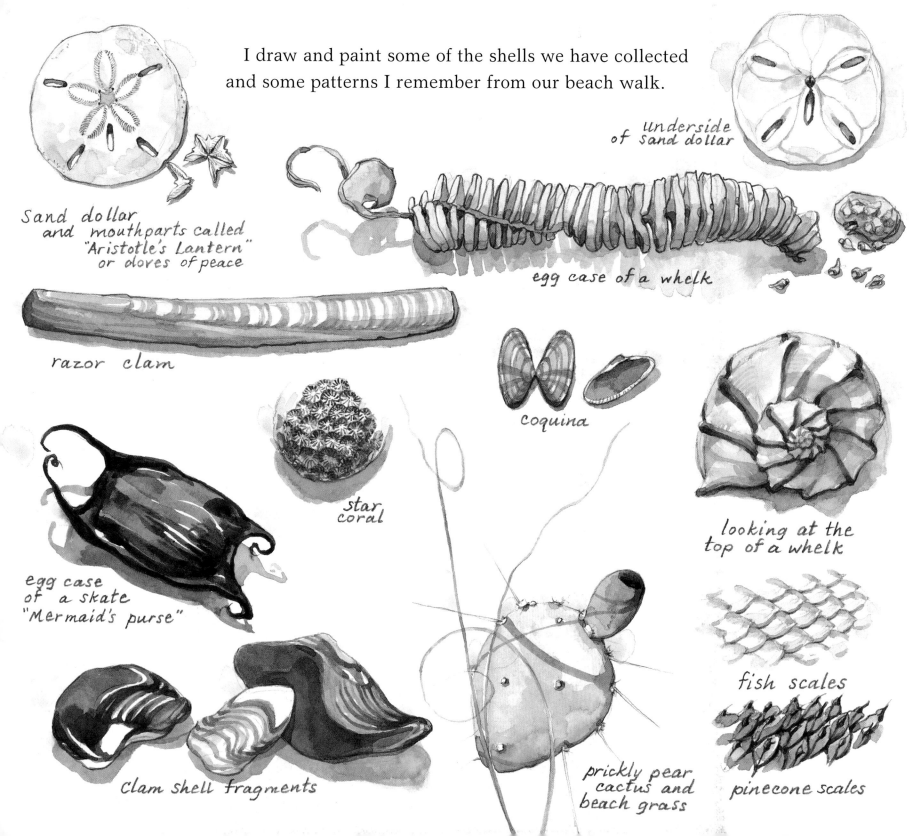

I draw and paint some of the shells we have collected and some patterns I remember from our beach walk.

Sand dollar and mouthparts called "Aristotle's Lantern" or doves of peace

underside of sand dollar

egg case of a whelk

razor clam

coquina

star coral

egg case of a skate "Mermaid's purse"

looking at the top of a whelk

Clam shell fragments

prickly pear cactus and beach grass

fish scales

pinecone scales

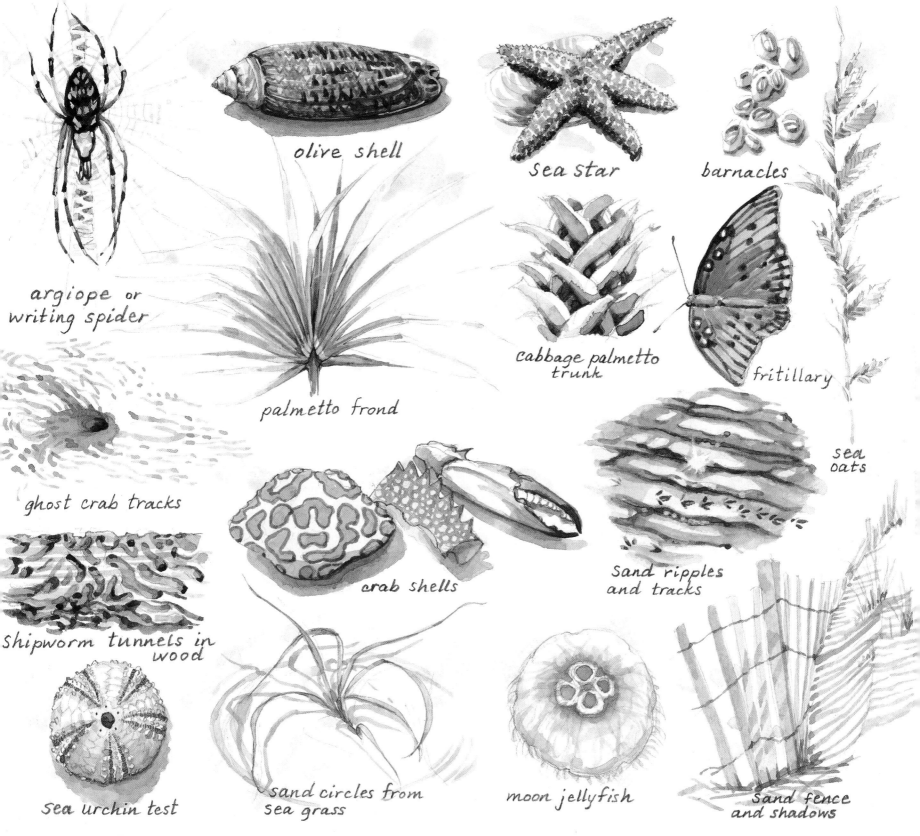

argiope or
writing spider

olive shell

sea star

barnacles

cabbage palmetto
trunk

fritillary

palmetto frond

sea
oats

ghost crab tracks

crab shells

Sand ripples
and tracks

Shipworm tunnels in
wood

sea urchin test

sand circles from
sea grass

moon jellyfish

Sand fence
and shadows

While I finish drawing, Amy packs a surprise lunch. We walk out to the dock to eat, sharing our crusts with some gulls. Amy sees a large black bird diving into the marsh water and looks it up in the bird book: a double-crested cormorant.

DOUBLE-CRESTED CORMORANT

Adult drying wings
L 27" W 50"

When I first came to the island, I used to walk along with my painting bag until I found a beautiful natural arrangement of shells and shadows, maybe a feather or a sand dollar. I would plop down and paint it, my only rule being I couldn't touch a thing. I called these paintings "found still lifes" and sometimes I painted large oils on canvas from them, back in my studio.

Amy stays on the dock to read and I walk along the marsh to the river. I always feel like I will find something just ahead, and often I do.

Once I found a fossil shark's tooth on the ocean beach.

Once I found some false teeth sticking up out of the sand! I have heard of people losing them overboard when they get seasick.

One day I was painting with a class near the egret pond. One of the students pointed out a huge alligator crawling out of the pond behind me (as if I had asked it to show up to model for us!)

A second later:
We cleared out so fast, I think we scared the poor alligator as much as it had scared us! We decided to paint at the beach instead of the pond that day.

I see a black skimmer
burst from her nest, faking
a broken wing to distract
me from her three small,
speckled eggs. She flops and
falls and limps, leading me
away, then flies back, just
fine, to sit on her nest again
after I hurry past.

A month ago I came upon a dead baby whale washed up
on the beach. When I called my naturalist friend to report
it, she told me it was a baby sperm whale. Scientists had
already studied it to learn why it had died. Its stomach had
contained a marine oil bottle, nylon rope, a black plastic
trash bag, a plastic buoy, and some rubber and Styrofoam.
The whale had starved because there was no room for food.

When I come back to our dock, I find some very mysterious footprints in the sand. Each print has toenails of jingle shells. The prints lead right to the house, where I find Amy inside writing some kind of list. We both stretch out to read during the hot Indian summer afternoon.

Things that wreck the beach
Natural
·erosion
·hurricanes
·flooding
·tsunamis
·animals (overpopulation of one species)
·red tide
Un
·dogs - bark, dig up dunes
·people - walk on dunes, build houses, cut down trees, step on plants + crabs + eggs
·oil spills
·pollution - trash dumped into water, toxic waste/sewage
·motor boats - leak gas, scare animals, run over sea turtles + whales
·cars - drive on dunes, smush turtles

At sunset, we walk back through the forest to the pond. Egrets are flying soundlessly down to roost in the live oaks, squawking only if one lands too close to another's sleeping spot. Soon there are so many it looks like snow has fallen on the trees. Amy counts 150 egrets, and one alligator in the middle of the pond leaving an S-shaped trail behind its powerful tail as it slowly circles in the dark water.

We race each other down the forest path to the beach. Reaching the dunes, we see a small group of people working to clear a path to the water . . . the baby loggerhead sea turtles are hatching!

Dangers to Sea Turtles

Birds

lights

Fishing line + nets

Trash: (plastic bags and balloons look like their favorite food... jellyfish)

sharks

ghost crabs

cats

foxes + raccoons

motor boats

cars

people

A Sea Turtle's Diet

Portuguese man-of-war

jellyfish

fish

squid

crab

shrimp

sea grass

mollusks

horseshoe crab

Sea turtle hatchlings always move toward light. If there are bright lights from motels, parking lots, and homes behind them, they will head away from the ocean and soon die on the dunes or roads. On the darkest nights, if there is no light, the babies still go toward the water. Do they hear the waves or smell the ocean? Do they follow the slope of the beach to the water? Are they guided by the Earth's magnetic field?

Dug from this Loggerhead
Nesting Site:

107 empty eggshells
4 rotten eggs
3 live hatchlings...
(They were carried near
the ocean, then allowed to
crawl in. This "imprinting"
enables the females to
return to the same beach
in about 25 years to lay
their eggs!)
    Males will spend their
lives in the ocean.
    The temperature of the
nest determines whether
the hatchlings are male
or female!

Three days after a hatching, naturalists come
back to excavate the nest. They count the empty
egg shells and rescue any weak hatchlings that may
not have made it to the surface. Only a licensed
naturalist is allowed to touch a sea turtle or an egg
or a nesting site.

Amy and I watch as the last of these little loggerheads
push their way to the ocean, are tumbled back to shore
by the waves, then finally swim out to deeper waters.
    We head quietly back to our cottage.

Tomorrow when we walk out to the ocean, the tide will have swept clean the shells and tracks from today. We will look at the ocean surface, broken by a fin from below or a boat or diving bird from above. Only traces of the hidden undersea world will wash up on the beach again: shells, bones and teeth, a jellyfish, a skate egg case . . . We want to look deeper below the shining surface, to walk farther along the shoreline, to stay longer at our island home.

willet

river otter

hermit crab

lugworm

cardinal

blue jay

goldenrod spider

white-tailed deer

black racer

Carolina anole

yellowthroat

hairstreak

marsh rice rat

red-bellied woodpecker

fish crow

brown thrasher

Carolina mantis

yellow-bellied turtle